THAT WEEK

NOT A MEMORY TO MEMORIZE

DHATREE SUNEETH
MARADANA

"To those who never give up no matter what."

Contents

Foreword

It was never easy to understand life sometimes. It gets so confusing that everything we wish to happen turns out to be a rare possibility. Closing my eyes, I smiled, seeing the darkness for the first time not because I was happy, it's because of the beauty that darkness carries in our life where we think everything is bright as light.

The Story is all about the darkness that life pushes us into without giving us any hint of how dark life will be.

Breaking free of darkness isn't easy, but we need to keep believing in our strength to find a way no matter what.

'Life isn't easy; it's not very difficult either.'

This is not just a book about Love but pain.

Pain that can keep messing with you as long as you keep breathing, pain that never ends, the pain that makes us numb, lost, and even triggers you to get mad at yourself.

Pain makes us suffer. It also makes us strong as we fight ourselves daily to live another day.

In the end it's you who're everyone and everything you want.

People stay but how long?

This is a story about you, my reader who always fights with the darkness in this world to live anothere day.

Acknowledgements

Thank you, Kundana, my friend and editor, for all my past stories, along with this, my first novel, for making it flawless.

Thank you, Mom, for believing in me. I know, dad, you're watching me as I write and smile thinking about you. Thankyou you for everything. Thankyou, brother, my friend Srinivas, who was more excited to read my stories before I could even finish them.

Special thanks to my friends who bear with me for all the texts I have sent them about the idea of a story, and you guys are the best critics!

Thanks to the flow of my thoughts and my words that always stay and travel with me through thick and thin of my life.

Thanks to you, my reader, for believing that my simple words can form a story and make the fiction breathe with the emotions we humans feel.

Note: The story and the characters are fictional, but the emotions you feel aren't.

EVERYONE has an incident that'll change them completely. The change that they never even thought of, expected or imagined. It's not just loving a person that changes you. There are a lot of other things besides love. The situations that surround you, people beside you, betrayal you experience and a lot more. We have hundreds of thoughts and aspirations, but how many do we even try to achieve? We hope to achieve everything we dream of, but how much do we work to achieve them?

Even I have a lot of aspirations that we dreamt of.

Yes. It's us... She and I.

Everything was going well but every time was not our time.

Life, right! It's a mixture of happiness and sadness. Balanced. Never imbalanced.

It's not just my story. It's gonna be the story of you. Yes, you! You have a lot of aspirations. Everyone does.

I don't know why we ended up like this. It's not about her. She still loves me. We're still together. We'll be until the end but.....

*

As in most of the love stories, I'm the one who proposed to her first. She's the only one who never judged me. I feel safe and secure in her company.

I'm a man who was an 'Introvert' and never got social or close to people. They called me a nerd for not getting social. But I didn't bother because I don't want to mess with someone and end up with wounds and pain. Not again. If you had noticed the word 'again', you're right... I got betrayed once and I don't want to undergo it again. Maybe it's not my mistake but I'm the one who's suffering due to the past. I want to tell you the whole story of mine, which made me an Introvert who's deeply hurt and lost everything except life. Maybe I gained a few things too.

Let me first tell you about the past. How I used to be once. Not a nerd, then.

I was a cool guy who's friendly with everyone, and I was the one girls craved for. That's what people around me said and I just had a sweet smile on my face whenever I heard that. I had a lot of friends among girls, with whom I never crossed the line. I was within my boundary and never loved anyone until she entered into my life. She was the girl every guy would crave for. How could I not fall for her, when she is the most beautiful girl in our entire college! I fell in love with her and got myself drowned deep into the ocean of love while holding her tight like we got our hands stuck together forever. We're happy together until that day. The day that ruined my life and tore me into pieces, making me an introvert, a nerd and what not. It's not just a single day, it was a horrible week that killed me inch by inch.

Of course, I'm alive now, but I'm not living. Just Breathing.

*

2

I was tired and was about to sleep when my mobile blinked as a message took my attention. It was her texting me late at night.

'Let's go out for a while, it read.

'Now?? Look at the time Chitti', I replied.

I was waiting for her reply but to my surprise, she called me. She never called me this late as her parents were too smart that they'll sense her talking. I picked up the call and sang.

'Hellooo chittiii... !'

I didn't hear anything except the rattling noise of the fan in her room.

I kept on saying.

'Hello...Hello... Chitti...?'

Expecting her to reply but, she has cut the call. I redialled her number.

It kept on ringing, but she didn't lift the call. I thought someone was around her and cut the call but little did I know that she was alone at her place that night as her parents were out of town and will return in the morning. I called her again and she had cut my call again. I was tired but I wanted to know what happened to her all of a sudden as she was asking me to meet her at this odd hour. But, I was very low on sleep due to my project work and on top of that,

I was disturbed by my friend's overreaction for rejecting his sister's love proposal to me. So, I threw my mobile aside and fell into my bed. Before drifting off to sleep, I gazed at my mobile for a moment expecting her call or message but there was none.

I was about to sleep when my mobile vibrated again. It's her call. I lifted the call and I heard her voice. She was in a panic.

'I don't know what's happening in my house. I'm afraid. Can you be here with me?' she almost cried.

I got up on my bed like a spring.

'Chitti... I... I'm coming... Don't worry,' I said, as I picked the keys running downstairs.

'What's the hurry?!' my mother asked.

'I'll text you when I reach the place,' I said, running towards the parking lot.

I kick-started the bike and drifted off as fast as I can. The speedometer showed 100kmph.

Everything is getting blurred to my eyes as sleep is taking control all over my senses. I slapped myself to control the sleep but I wasn't that successful.

'I came close to her house. I'll be there in just a couple of minutes,' I said out loud to keep myself awake.

All of a sudden, someone came running towards the bike. I applied the brakes at once. Due to the over-speed I was driving at, I lost control over my bike and my body was rolled over the road. I could see a person running towards me. It was a girl. I could see her indistinctly from a distance as I went unconscious.

*

By the time I woke up, my mother was beside me. She told me that it's been two days since I went unconscious.

'I'm fine mom.. see,' I said, raising my legs and hands simultaneously. I could see a slight smile as she saw me awake.

Parents love us as we are, as we were and whatever we become; because they're our parents. I opened my mobile to check the texts and calls that are left unattended. I flipped through the calls and texts but there were no messages or calls from her. I gave a fake smile to my mom who was watching me. I was thinking of Chitti, worried about what would have happened to her and why there was no message or a call from her. A shiver rolled down my spine as I assumed that something would have happened to her. My mom knew I searched for Chitti's message but she didn't react.

I texted her a 'Hy!'

I was feeling a bit drowsy and was unable to see clearly. My friend Raghav came to check up on me. I couldn't see him clearly but I have known him for the past 15 years. So, I can say it's him.

"How are you doing buddy ? " he asked me before he wished my mom.

"Fine," I muttered.

"Hie!" I heard a cheerful voice from his back.

It's his sister, Varsha.

"Hey!" I said.

"Will you guys be here," my mom asked.

"Yes auntie, we actually are here from the morning. I'll leave before lunch," Raghav said and added, "Auntie, you can go home. Varsha will be here till evening. I have to attend a few meetings in the afternoon. I'll drop by in the evening and pick up Varsha."

Raghav is my childhood friend and is a born billionaire. He knows everything about me as he's my closest friend to me, despite the fact that I have a lot of friends. Varsha knows that I'm already in love for a year now, but she proposed to me a month ago. I rejected her. From then Raghav and I barely spoke to each other as he frequently tried to convince me to marry Varsha. My mom knows that Varsha had a huge crush on me. Varsha told her parents that she loves me and her parents talked to my mom. So I couldn't keep it a secret anymore and had to tell my mom about my relationship. She did accept my relationship. Then she told Varsha's parents that she should talk to my dad when he returns from camp and then decides. However, I know my dad will be affirmative with my relationship. My mother handled the situation with care as words are the things that make people misunderstand each other.

Now, as I was lying on the hospital bed, Raghav somehow convinced my mother to go home and take a rest. She couldn't disagree with him as she stayed by my side without proper sleep for the past two days. Even I assured her that I'll be fine. Varsha led my mom and Raghav out of the hospital. I was not alone, but fear and anxiety were all over my head about her. My mobile didn't blink or vibrate.

I'm Dhatree and this is the beginning of the biggest disaster in my life. Maybe it already started but I didn't see it coming through.

*

My mother left for home and Raghav too left after a while. He was successful in executing his plan, leaving Varsha alone with me so that we could understand each other and he hoped we could have some private conversation. She was staring at me with full concentration as if she would eat me alive, while my concentration was somewhere else. I asked her to leave me alone to let me rest for a while. She didn't leave me, instead put her palm on mine which reminded me of Chitti.

'What?' I asked her in dismay.

'Nothing.... Hah! I love you,' she whispered, coming closer to my ear.

I couldn't take it. She knows everything and she's doing the same again and again.

'Varsha! I told you many times I don't have any feelings for you and moreover, I'm in a relationship. You know everything about it yet you still...' I paused before I could continue.

'We're apart but she is the only one whom I can actually think of now and all the time even when we're apart. To be frank, you're nice and you will definitely get a good guy, but not me. Chitti owns me. You are like a good friend to me and moreover my best friend's sister. I don't want you to get disheartened. I want you to stay as a good friend of mine who knows everything about me. I don't want to lose people who are like my family and who stay by my side when I need them. Please don't say those words again. I can't reflect the same feelings because they belong only to Chitti. I love her.‘

By the time I completed my words Varsha started getting emotional and tears rolled down her cheeks. This is not the first time she was crying in front of me but this time, I felt low seeing her cry. This time it was something different. Maybe she understood what I meant or she's trying to understand. I slowly patted her hand to console her, still thinking of Chitti.

Varsha gave a smile wiping her tears. I saw her face and she looked beautiful but I still don't know what happened to my beautiful Chitti.

Varsha promised me that she'll never talk about this again and assured me that she shall be a friend of mine.

Suddenly, it crossed my mind that I hit a girl the night I met with an accident.

Varsha caught me staring at my mobile and asked if something was bothering me. 'I hit a girl that night but I don't know who she is,' I muttered.

Varsha kept silent.

'And, I don't know what happened to Chitti. She is not responding to my texts or calls... I... I'm worried', I added.

She still kept silent.

'She went missing', Varsha blurted out the unknown truth.

Is this a dream or am I feeling drowsy due to the medicine that took off my senses making me hear something wrong?

After a little pause, she continued...

'She went missing that night when you met with the accident near her house, her parents who returned home the next day came to know about that and filed a complaint at the local PS. The investigation is being carried out. Her parents said that neither jewellery nor valuables were robbed. Police said that they found some clues and claimed that it's a kidnap,' she told everything she knew.

I couldn't move. There was total silence. I couldn't believe what she said. I could still remember that feeling. I felt as if time had stopped and my heart pumped high. I wanted to see her. I wanted to howl out loud. I wanted to get back to the past. I couldn't believe that she was kidnapped. I felt numb. I howled like hell inside my mind but it didn't get out of my throat. Everything felt like a war. My breath got heavier. The machine beside me kept beeping like a siren and the doctors rushed to my room. There were tears in my eyes. Doctors kept moving in and out checking my BP and were asking me to talk. I couldn't speak. I was clueless. I was given an injection. Before I could know what was happening my eyes got shut and my mind slept in silence. But, deep down I'm still thinking about who could have kidnapped Chitti and why would they kidnap Chitti.

I love you Chitti. I kept screaming in my head but I couldn't get up from the drowsiness. That injection worked for two more hours on me but my brain couldn't resist knowing what happened to Chitti.

*

'You need to rest for a while. The doctor said that you need to rest, so they can discharge you this evening,' Varsha helped me as I tried to get off the bed.

'Can I just go to the washroom on my own?' I asked her.

She laughed, 'Okay go.'

I locked myself in the washroom and dialled Chitti's number.

There's no response. I redialed and...

'Hello!' an unfamiliar voice lifted the call.

'Chitti..!' I said softly.

'I'm her mother beta. Who is this?' the lady said.

'Dhatree,' I mumbled.

'Dhatree. How are you? When did you get discharged? We came yesterday to see you?' her voice felt low as she was trying to act normal.

Before I could answer her questions, there was a knock on the door.

'Dhatree are you ok? The doctor is here,' Varsha shouted.

'Auntie I'm ok. Is there any clue about Chitti?' I asked, my voice shaking.

'Dhatree....' she kept sobbing.

'Is that true?' I asked her.

'Yes....' was the only answer from her.

How could she even talk more than those three words when her daughter went missing and no one knows whether she is safe or not.

I couldn't think any further. I cut the call and went out of the washroom.

'You ok?' the doctor asked.

'Yes...No....aah! I don't know.. doctor. I want to leave now. Can I ? I'm fine right? I feel a bit of pain in my head,' I asked him.

'You're fine. We'll discharge you in a few hours. Maybe the pain is because of the wound in your head. Nothing serious,' he smiled and left.

'Everything will be fine, Dhatree,' Varsha smiled.

'I don't know Varsha. What the fuck is happening? Who could take away Chitti from me? And, this accident to me is because of that girl... ' I stopped mid-sentence.

'That girl...' I mumbled.

Closing my eyes I tried to figure out what actually happened that night.

'You need to sleep for a while and eat your lunch first,' Varsha said, unwrapping the lunch box she brought.

'Can we go out? I want to feel the fresh air. I want to know what actually happened,' I said while eating lunch.

'You need to sleep,' Vasha smiled.

'No! I don't want to fucking sleep here and think of what happened to Chitti. I want to know what happened. It's ok if you're not coming. I'm fine and I can go,' I shouted.

'You just relax. Ok, we'll go. I need to inform the doctor before we leave,' she said getting up.

I don't know who was the girl that hit me. Is she fine?

If she's not the one who admitted me to the hospital, who admitted me?

If she was hurt, she should be in the hospital. I went out of my room and searched the other rooms if I could find a girl. I found a little girl who was being diagnosed with cancer. Her mother looked like my mother when I was a kid.

'Can I know who admitted me to the hospital?' I asked at the reception desk.

'You here?' Varsha said coming towards me.

'Just came to check who admitted me,' I said, waiting for the receptionist to answer me.

'It was a girl, sir. She didn't mention her name. She admitted you and left,' the receptionist said.

'Chitti?' I mumbled.

'When did she leave? Did she say anything?' I asked her curiously.

'Ahhh!!! She said she was your girlfriend. She said she'll be back in a while and left,' the receptionist said.

'Didn't she come back? ' I said more to myself.

'Sir my shift was done that night and I left early. I don't know,' she said.

'I need to know where Chitti is,' I shouted, banging the table.

'We'll find her. Police are doing their part. You need to rest,' Varsha said, trying to console me by putting her palm on my shoulder as we went back to the room.

'Fuck rest! I don't want any rest. I want to know about Chitti. My Chitti is missing and it's been around three days and I'm sitting in this hospital without even trying to find her,' I screamed, pushing her hand away.

'Calm down Dhatree. The doctor said he'll discharge you at 4 in the evening. You need to take a rest,' Varsha said.

'I don't want any rest. I'm fucking awesome. Please don't treat me like I'm a patient and tell me everything you know about Chitti,' I said out loud, losing my temper.

'I don't know much of what happened. But, her parents said there were few mud footprints in their house, the police collected the samples and said it was two different people. One was yours...'

I was stunned.

'Mine?' I asked her, shocked.

'Yes,' she mumbled.

'WTF! I was met with an accident at the end of her street and fell unconscious. How could one of the food prints be mine? What about the other? ' I asked, confused.

'I don't know,' she mumbled.

'Fuck! what just happened that night?!' I shouted.

'What's happening to me,' I said and caught my head trying to remember what happened.

'Everything will be fine with time Dhatree,' Varsha came closer to me.

'No please...leave me alone,' I waved her away.

She didn't talk. She walked out of the room, closing the door from behind.

*

'I told you not to think of those days again and again,' Chitti's voice broke my thoughts.

'I still don't understand why I feel the pain of those horrible days though it's been a year,' I asked, taking a cup of coffee from her.

'Because that changed our lives forever. It made you suffer for months. It ruined everything we had,' Chitti said, sipping the coffee.

'You're right... I should get over it. Don't you think I'm getting back to the old Dhatree these days,' I smiled at her.

'Yes you are, but remember, if you flirt with someone I'll kick your ass,' Chitti said.

We both laughed.

'We're together now. We'll always be as we promised to each other,' I smiled.

'I love you,' she said.

'I love you too,' I whispered in her ears, hugging her from behind.

'How's the office going?' she asked, leaving into the kitchen.

'It's going good. Today I saw him,' my voice trailed away.

'Whom?' she asked from the kitchen.

I remained silent and went back to the past wondering why he had done that to us.

*

'I'm sorry,' I said to Varsha for shouting at her a while ago.

She came back as I had to take my medicines.

'I can understand,' she said, giving me my tablets.

'Thank you,' I smiled back.

I felt a bit relieved after having my medicine. I still have to wait for an hour more to get discharged.

'We'll go to the Police Station and then to her house to find out everything about Chitti,' she said, smiling at me.

" I'll go. You head back home and take mom along with you," I insisted.

'You need help. I can come. Raghav will accompany auntie to home,' she said.

'You're a girl and I don't want you to come along,' I tried to convince Varsha.

'I'm coming with you and it's final,' she hushed.

I agreed.

'Is there something more I need to know about Chitti? ' I asked her.

'Ahh...!!! Yes..!' she said.

'What?' I asked curiously.

'She got the best partner,' Varsha smiled.

'I hope she's fine. I miss her. I want to see her now,' my eyes went moist.

'We'll find her,' she held my hand comforting me.

*

After an hour, I was discharged and was asked to take my medicines whenever I felt stressed or pain in my head and some had a time period.

'What actually happened to me?' I asked my mom when she came out from the doctor's cabin.

'Nothing beta. you're fine,' she said trying to hide her expressions with a smile.

'If I'm fine, why am I supposed to have these medicines daily?' I raised my eyebrow.

'Oh! This is just a medical course for a few weeks to make you feel better. There's nothing to worry and don't overthink,' she smiled as I got up to leave.

Varsha was already waiting with Raghav at the entrance.

'Maa! Varsha and I have few things to do. We'll leave,' I said, signalling Varsha.

'You're going to meet Chitti's parents right?' maa said.

'I want to know what happened maa. I love her. Why is my footprint there? She is the one who admitted me to the hospital. Now she's gone missing and how can I do nothing to find her. I can't live with this maa. This kills me. Thinking she'll come back but doing nothing to find her. They're saying it's a kidnap, but there isn't a call from the kidnapers,' I frowned at her.

'I understand beta but don't forget to have your tablets. Come back soon,' She sighed.

She's not willing to send me but she knows that I'm not going to listen to her.

'Raghav will drop you home. Varsha and I will join you for dinner at 9,' I smiled at her.

'If one of my footprints was there, why didn't the police come to me?' I asked Varsha as we took a cab for the PS.

'They did come for you. But...' the car halted at the PS and we got down.

'Aditya!' I stood there shocked.

*

Aditya is Chitti's cousin. He is a police officer. I met him many times as he was transferred to Vijayanagaram and he comes to Vizag every weekend to meet his parents. I still remember the first time I met Aditya.

Chitti and I love long drives. We were on the way to Bheemili beach as it was the weekend and he was on duty at a place checking vehicles. I had everything except the pollution clearance.

I don't know why they need a pollution clearance for a vehicle though it was just a year ago I bought it. Chitti saw him from a distance and waved to him.

*

'Dhatree! You're ok right!', Aditya asked me as I kept thinking while Aditya and Varsha were discussing the case details.

'He keeps getting lost in thoughts whenever he thinks of Chitti. He's thinking too much,' Varsha said.

'You here?' I asked Aditya.

'I requested the local PS that I would take up Chitti's missing case so that I can find her soon,' he said.

'I want to help you. I want my Chitti,' I said with bulging eyes that looked red.

I don't know why my eyes looked red. Might be anger or tears. Maybe both mixed up.

'I should not involve the suspects in the crime but you're not the suspect,' he said.

Varsha and I looked at him shocked.

'Do you remember anything that happened that night?' Aditya asked, looking at me.

'I fell off my bike as a girl came onto my bike suddenly. Before I went unconscious seeing that girl running towards me. I tried to get up but she kept saying something. I don't remember clearly,' I said, closing my eyes and thinking about what happened to me that day.

The pain started in my head as I kept thinking.

'I guess I can't remember. It's painful,' I said and caught my head.

'You need to rest. Maybe it's because of Epilepsy. You can't stress too much,' Varsha said, holding me by the shoulders.

'What? Epi...sy what's that? Maa said that I'm normal,' I raised my voice.

'Nothing serious. You need to think less. I mean.. don't stress your mind. It's because of the little wound in your brain that occurred when you fell off the bike and hit the pole,' she said.

'I know what Epilepsy means. Don't act smart. Maybe I lost a little part of the memory that I couldn't figure out. Wait... What did you say? A pole?' I asked her.

'Yes! You hit a pole and so the injury occurred,' she said looking at me.

'No! I didn't hit a pole. I fell beside the road and there's no pole at that side of the road. All the poles are in the middle of that road,' I said, still thinking.

'The injury occurred with a rusted iron pole or rod. There are traces of rust near the wound. The doctor told us after the treatment,' Varsha said thoughtfully.

'The second Footprint,' I mumbled.

'I think we should check at Chitti's house if we can find any other clues. Maybe you can remember something,' Aditya said.

On the way I heard Aditya talking over the call about the cocaine smuggling in the shape of ivory from the Andhra Orissa border, Paralakhemundi.

It is Chitti's birthplace. I still remember all the things we explored at her town when I went to meet her family once.

I loved her family when we first met at Simhachalam. The vibe they gave made me feel like Family. I loved her mom. She was so joyful and made me feel free. Dads are a bit typical so is her father. It took time for me to get to know her dad. Not a long time though. In our second meeting, the next day I made my mark.

'Go, have a puff with my dad,' Chitti winked.

'What? You want to go to the washroom?' her mother asked.

'No maa. He wants to go to dad,' she giggled.

I looked at her. She laughed and her mom joined her.

'Very Funny,' I said, slapping her hand under the table.

The next meet with her parents is at her place in Paralakhemundi.

I loved the ivory works at her house. Maybe when we love someone I think we love everything about them, we also love their family, the house they live in and everything related and connected to their life because they're sharing their life with us.

Madhu Mahadev Shiv Mandir.

I love this temple as it is surrounded by the Sita Sagar lake on the three sides and the view looks fascinating in the evening with the sun drifting to it's horizon painting the water greenish orange. The birds retreating to their tiny nests makes it even beautiful. That place became so special for me not only because of the scenic beauty but also because she told her family about us there.

And, yes there was a discussion for a while in Hindi so that I couldn't understand all of it. Except for the change in their facial expressions.

For a while I felt like Krish in two states and Chitti is Ananya who's convincing her family and smiling at me.

Later they agreed with a smile.

There's no Hindi smile or Telugu smile. A smile doesn't need a language. It is always a smile. It always reflects positivity.

They welcomed me into their family with a hug. A warm family hug.

I felt so happy that they accepted us. Our Love.

My parents already know about her and agreed about us being lovers for now and my better half in a few months or years.

We just needed to settle down in life.

But, all of our dreams are shattered now. She's missing and I have this epilepsy.

*

'Fuckkk...!' I screamed.

'What happened? ' Aditya stopped the car.

'This is the place I fell off my bike,' I said, getting out of the car.

There's no pole or any rock. We have to travel 250 meters to her house.

I kept thinking of what would have happened.

I could remember everything getting blurry. I closed my eyes sitting at the place I met with the accident and kept trying to figure out what happened to me.

My head started to ache again but I didn't stop thinking.

'There's a van parked right opposite to her house,' I said.

'Yes! I collected the CCTV footage at her house that day. The van left after 3 AM that day and I don't know if Chitti is home after admitting you at the hospital. I need to check the hospital parking footage,' Aditya called one of the constables to bring the footage to Chitti's house.

I walked slowly to her house if I could remember anything while Varsha accompanied me and Aditya kept driving slowly behind us.

'Chitti!' I mumbled as I kept thinking of her.

Tears rolled down my cheeks and my legs felt too weak even to move a step. My head felt heavier and heavier with every passing second. I kept gasping for air.

Panic attack. I fell on my knees and went unconscious.

Varsha held me and helped me get into the car.

I felt like I was experiencing the same scenario that night.

I woke up in Chitti's room after 30 minutes. I looked at her mother who kept crying.

'You'll be fine Dhatree,' she said, putting her hand on my forehead.

I smiled looking at her.

I woke up and suddenly I noticed something in her room.

'What's that,' I asked Chitti's mother, pointing at the idol.

'Oh! That's an Ivory carving from our ancestors,' she said.

'Ivory carving..' I mumbled more to myself.

'What?' Aditya asked curiously.

I closed my eyes trying to remember about that night.

'When I fell off the bike I said that a girl came running towards me, right?

That's not Chitti. She's her friend Smitha. Her house is on the next street so I asked her to check on Chitti before I reached them.

She said something about ivory when I went unconscious.

We need to talk to her,' I said, getting up as quickly as possible.

*

'What happened that night?' I asked Smitha.

' I'm sorry. I was afraid to tell the truth. I wanted to come to you and talk about it but I thought that you would misunderstand me. That's the reason why I said my name as Chitti at the hospital's reception desk. I never thought that she would go missing," she cried out loud.

'Tell me what exactly happened,' Aditya stammered.

'After Dhatree called, I went to her house. I saw her shouting at someone and went into her room. On seeing me, she started shouting, asking me to run away. As I looked around, there's a man there. He saw me and came running behind me. That's how I hit you while he was chasing me. I came running to you. I saw her talking about ivory works. The man hit you with an iron rod and you fell off. Chitti came screaming and he ran towards her. Take him away she screamed and diverted him to the other road and I drove you to the hospital and admitted you. When I came back to check on Chitti, she's gone. The doors are unlocked. I went in. She's not there, a shiver ran in me and I drove home without telling anyone. I know you'll come and see me so I waited,' she said, still sobbing.

'Can you identify the man?' Aditya asked.

'I can try to,' she said.

'Ok, I'll arrange for an artist to draw his sketch tomorrow morning. You should come to the station tomorrow,' Aditya said and got up to leave.

'Yes. Sure sir,' she said.

Aditya and Varsha went ahead of me and I was about to leave the house then Smitha came running to me with a book.

'This is the book she gave me that night. Don't let anyone know about this, not even the people with you,' she said.

'Remember, sometimes people whom you believe are the best, give you the worst betrayal,' she added.

I smiled at her and put the book in my jacket's pocket so that no one could see it.

*

5

As promised to my mom. Varsha and I were at home by 9 for dinner.

'You can stay for tonight,' mom asked her.

'No auntie. I already called Raghav to pick me up. He might be on his way,' Varsha said.

Raghav came and Varsha left with him.

I went to my mother's room and kept talking about the case details till late at night.

'Why do you love her so much?' She asked.

'Should there be a reason to love someone with whom you dreamt of a new world and with whom you would love to spend your remaining life with?' I asked her.

She didn't speak and turned to the other side.

'Mom, I love her. Dad and you accepted that. Now she's missing. I want her back. I'm going to find her at any cost,' I said, getting up to leave.

'I know you love her,' she said.

'When is dad coming?' I asked, ignoring the topic.

'I don't know. He said he has got some urgent meeting to attend,' she closed her eyes pretending to sleep.

I went into my room and shut the door.

It was around 12:00 AM.

'Don't let anyone know about this,' Smitha's words flashed to my head.

'Where is the book,' I mumbled while searching for it.

'Where the fuck is it!' I screamed.

I kept thinking of where I would have kept it.

My jacket.

I rushed downstairs and there's my jacket.

The book is safe.

I went back to my room and locked myself.

That is the journal I gifted her on her birthday. I love the way she writes the true feelings. She pretends to be fine all the time faking herself but after she met me it was different. I made it different.

I opened the journal.

Nearly half of the journal was written by me about us. She wanted to read my journal so I wrote it for her. I kept flipping through the pages I got reminded of all the nights I kept writing about the day how I felt about her. The way she loved me.

I quickly flipped to the last page and my mobile buzzed.

Varsha was the caller's name.

I checked the time. It was 1:00AM.

I lifted the call. She cut the call. I thought it was by mistake and turned towards the journal.

My mobile buzzed again. It was not Varsha.

It's an unknown caller.

I lifted the call.

'Dhatree... Dhatree... It's me, Varsha. Dhatree... hello.. meet me now... it's so important. It's about Ch...itti... I'm running towards your house. They might kill me. I'll hide my mobile,' the call got disconnected.

I rushed out of my room taking the car keys. I raced towards her house.

With the pacing speed, my mind was racing with a lot of thoughts.

Who are they?

What is Varsha talking about?

Why would they kill her?

What is it about Chitti?

'I can't lose anyone,' I said out loud, hitting the accelerator hard.

I saw her running towards me. I slowed down and hit the break.

I went running to her. There's no one behind her.

She came walking slowly towards me and fell off.

I lifted her. There's blood on her back.

'Varsha... Varsha...' I kept calling her.

She's slowly going unconscious. I took her to the car and drifted off to the hospital.

'Varsha please hold on... you'll be fine.

'Varsha, nothing will happen to you,' I said, trying to keep her conscious.

She kept mumbling Chitti's name all the way.

I took her to my friend who's a doctor.

She disagreed first to get the treatment as it's a risk if the police find out.

She later agreed because the doctor is my friend from childhood and her name is Chandrika.

If it's not your best friend, who will help you in your crisis.

I fell off thinking what would have happened to Chitti and what would have happened to Varsha if I was not on time.

'You need not keep stressing yourself,' Chandrika said as I woke up after an hour.

'Ok Doctor Ji but I need to find Chitti,' I said, getting up.

'You can't go now. Varsha needs bed rest at least for two days,' she said.

'Can I talk to her?' I asked.

'Only tomorrow morning,' Chandrika said, gesturing to rest.

'I need to go home. Don't tell anyone about Varsha and me coming to your place,' I said leaving.

'You need to have your dosage,' Chandrika suggested.

'I'm fine,' I said walking away.

I needed that dose badly as my head kept aching for a while. But Chitti is what I need now, not the dosage.

I rode back home. It's already 5:00 AM. I went slowly into my room and found the journal missing.

'Fuckkk!' I screamed.

I searched for it. I ran back to the car. It's there.

I kept breathing heavily as I went back to my room.

I took the dosage of my anti-epileptic drugs and fell on my bed holding the journal in my hand.

I flipped through the pages and found some strange note which looked mysterious.

That was written,

'Rouy dad si a gurd relaed. Eh setah em. Idnumehkalarap atis ragas'

I couldn't understand it. I searched in google but I couldn't find it.

I kept staring at these words.

I don't know how to crack it.

Staring at the words I felt like I needed help.

My head started to ache again.

I started to gaze at those words which looked like an unsolved puzzle.

Wait, what? I mumbled to myself seeing the second word.

Dad?

I reversed the word, it's still dad.

I started to re-write every word.

'Your dad is a drug dealer. He hates me. Paralakhemundi Sita Sagar'.

'What the fuck..!' I screamed. I tried calling my dad.

He didn't pick up. I could hear some words in Oriya.

'Apana jeun byakti nku call karuchanthi se tara ittara deu nahanti, dayankari kicchi samaya pare chesta karantu'

I kept calling my dad, but he didn't pick up. The same lady said those words in Oriya again and again.

*

It's 7 AM in the morning and mom was making breakfast. And my eyes looked pale without sleep. I felt weak and my head kept aching.

'Maybe I should go to Paralakhemundi,' I whispered to myself.

Sometimes it's not about should, it's a must.

But what should I tell mom?

I need to see how Varsha is. Taking the car keys and my wallet I told mom that I'm going to meet my new investors in Hyderabad. I packed my bag and the medicines which I need the most.

There were a row of questions from her after listening to my words. Answering them with utmost care I left the house.

*

6

'How is she?' I asked Chandrika about Varsha on the call.

'She needs rest. She just got up. I'll tell the maid to take care of her and leave for the hospital by 9,' she said.

'Okay! Listen to me carefully. Don't let anyone know about Varsha. I'm going to Paralakhemundi. I found a clue. I think I'm close to finding Chitti,' I said crossing Yendada Junction.

I stopped my car when I saw a little girl crying on the roadside.

I walked up to her and asked her name.

'Ishitha,' she said, still crying.

'Chitti,' I mumbled.

Chitti's actual name was Ishitha. I love to call her Chitti. That's what you do when you love someone. You give them a nickname that only you can call, no one else.

The girl stopped crying as she saw someone approaching us.

'Can you help me change the tyre? My sir is waiting in the car,' he asked me.

He himself looked like he could lift a car with his bare hands.

I looked at the opposite of the road where his car stopped.

'Dad,' I mumbled to myself and turned to the man.

'Sorry, sir I need to go urgently. The girl is crying so I stopped here just to make sure the girl is fine,' I said, asking the girl to get in so that I could drop her.

I needed an excuse for now. Before my dad could see I faded into the traffic.

'Uncle my house is here,' the little girl said at Madhurawada.

'Uncle?' I said to myself.

I stopped the car and went to her house.

'Where did you go? What's that on your cheeks?' her mother came running to her.

'Uncle gave me a chocolate,' she giggled, wiping off the chocolate on her cheeks.

'I'm sorry. She has this habit of walking away alone,' her mother said.

'She's a kid. You need to take care of her. The little flaw as a kid becomes a danger when she grows up,' I said and turned to leave.

'I didn't go alone. My dad took me,' the little girl said.

'Then why're you left alone?' I asked her.

Her mother kept silent.

'What happened?' I asked softly.

'Bhai, my husband, is a drug addict. Not only him, but also there are a lot of people who are addicted to cocaine,' she paused.

The thought of cocaine made me think of the man behind this. My dad. I can't think that he's doing this because he has had the greed for money for a long time. But by ruining lives?

'Bhai please don't tell anyone about cocaine because it will affect us,' she pleaded.

'I won't tell. But where is your husband?' I asked.

'He might have gone to Rushikonda and forgot that he took the girl along with him. We're used to this. This is not the first time he left her alone. She used to go with my husband and come back late as someone who knows her would drop her. Thankyou Bhai!' She said weeping.

I smiled leaving the house.

I started with the thought of bringing back Chitti but now I have something more to it,Cocaine.

Is my Dad a Drug dealer!? How could he hide it from me all these years? He said it's a Logistics company yet this feels weird and crazy to hear all of a sudden that my dad facked what he did to cover up his illegal business.

I removed my sim card and took the sim I borrowed from Chandrika. So if I remove my sim before I cross the Andhra Border, everyone who calls me could only listen to Telugu words saying that my number is switched off and not the Oriya words.

Checking the directions on Google maps, I called Arpita.

Arpita is Chitti's best friend in Paralakhemundi. I know I can't manage myself because the more I think, the heavier my head aches. And, it's been so long since I had seen her.

I never had a sister. So when she called me 'Annaya' (brother in Telugu) for the first time, I got emotionally connected with her. I called Chitti and cried out loud that Arpita called me 'Annaya'. Maybe that's the magic in the mother tongue. When someone calls you with relation we get connected easily feeling that they are our family.

We boys look hard, but we too are humans and we do have emotions and feelings. We never show them much, but sometimes we can never control them. Mostly at nights and in the dark when no one is watching, we cry out loud, pouring out all the pain and anger into tears from our eyes.

'Hello! This is Dhatree,' I said.

'Annayaaa!' she squealed.

She doesn't know anything about Chitti. I don't want to let her know until I get there. She would be worried.

'Arpi, I'm coming to Paralakhemundi. I need a favour,' I said, sounding normal.

'Seriously? You're coming. What happened to that idiot? She has not picked up the call for three days. She didn't even check my messages. Everything is fine right?' she enquired.

'Nothing is fine, chelli,' is what I wanted to say.

But I ended up saying, 'Yeah fine chelli! She is busy as it's the end of the financial year.'

'Yeah, Annaya! You need to take care of her. She's such a workaholic,' she said.

'Is there any work here?' she asked.

'Yeah, I need to visit the temple near Sita Sagar. Dad had someplace over there. And, remember chelli, don't let anyone know that I'm coming. I'll explain to you once I'm there,' I said and hung up.

As I kept moving towards my destination my thought's kept racing. I know I need to rest more and think less but, Chitti matters to me the most. Finding her and knowing what happened to her matters the most.

Driving through Srikakulam I kept thinking of the times we used to go on long drives and have our favourite Biryani with Sprite at Foresta Restaurant.

'I love biryani with Sprite,' she said enjoying the food.

'You said you love me,' I giggled.

'Well... I love both,' she said, still enjoying the food.

No one can stop her from eating her biriyani, not even her favourite actor.

Even if her favourite actor was here and she wanted to meet him, she would say,

'Ask him to wait. I need to finish my biriyani.'

Well, I'm no different from her because biriyani love for both of us is endless.

As I kept thinking my eyes started to get blurred.

I wanted to stop. I crossed Meliaputti a few minutes ago and just 8 kilometres away from Paralakhemundi.

I can manage... I can manage... Don't think much... I said to myself forgetting that I haven't taken my medicines after falling off at Chandrika's place.

I slowed down the car moving to my extreme left and stopped.

I got down to wash my face. Taking the water bottle from the backpack I found a cover in the seat pocket.

I opened it and read.

'What the fuck!' I screamed after reading all that.

There was fear all over my body. My head was hurting like hell. I took the tablets and tried to control my thoughts. I kept inhaling and exhaling slowly to control myself.

Focus...focus I said to myself, closing my eyes and washing my face.

I took the high dosage and started off as it's already 1 PM.

*

I called Arpita to send me the location.

Within the next twenty minutes, I'm at her house thinking of how to tell her about Chitti.

'What are you thinking Ananya?' Arpita came out of the kitchen with some snacks.

'Nothing chelli. Just some work stuff,' I said, faking a smile.

'New Spectacles?' she said, smiling at me.

'Her gift chelli. She gave as I love capturing moments. This has a spy camera,' I said, still thinking how to tell her about Chitti.

'What happened to Chitti?' she asked, placing the plate on the table and looking at me.

'Nothing Chelli. She's busy at work. How is your life going?' I tried to divert the topic.

'I called auntie and she told me everything,' Arpita whispered.

I kept silent thinking about what to say and what to say.

'Annaya!' Arpita said, clasping my hand.

My head was burning with all the thoughts and the letter in the cover made me think too much which I shouldn't do.

My eyes started to get blurred as I took out the cover from my pocket.

Handing it to Arpita, I fell on the floor. My head kept rotating as she kept yelling Annaya...Annaya... but I couldn't tell anything. I pointed to my backpack and my eyes closed.

Everything went black.

*

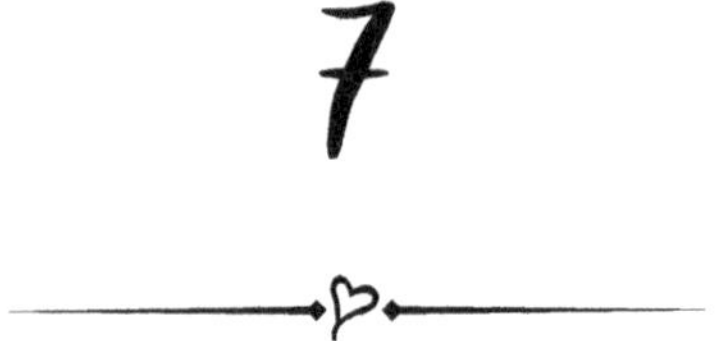

Arpita sat beside me reading the paper I gave her before I went unconscious.

I don't know how many times she read it. The content in the paper demands us to read it again and again.

'Annaya! Are you ok?' she asked.

'I'm feeling better Chelli. I have been affected with epilepsy for a few days now,' I mumbled getting up from the bed.

'From the day Chitti went missing right?' she asked, looking at me.

'Yes! Everything is fucked up. I need to find Chitti. The only clue I have is Sita Sagar. I need to go and search for her,' I said, waking up from the bed.

'You need some rest annaya. I'm not allowing you to go now. Chitti is fine. Nothing will happen to her. This letter says it is annaya. Let my husband come, I'll ask him to accompany you,' Arpita said, stopping me from getting up from my bed.

'Chai,' an old lady said, bringing us tea and biscuits. It's her mother in law.

I smiled at her.

'You need some rest beta. Don't think much. Everything will be fine with time,' her mother in law said while serving tea.

Arpita's family knows Chitti and me very well from the day of Arpita's marriage. Being her best friend, Chitti was with Arpita from the day the marriage arrangements started. I ended up being a part of it because of Chitti. I still remember those three days.

'Can I meet Chitti?' I asked an old man.

'Chitti? Who's Chitti? Who are you?' he asked.

'I'm Chitti's friend. Is it Arpita's house?' I asked him.

'Ha Mera beti Arpita ka marriage. Who are you?' he asked, raising his eyebrow suspiciously as if I'm looking like a thief in my favourite red T-shirt with a batman symbol on it. That's my favourite T-shirt. Apparently, that's Chitti's gift.

'Oh, uncle Ji. I'm Arpita's best friend ka mangetar,' I smiled, shaking his hands.

'She doesn't have a friend with the name Chitti. You Idiot,' he shouted.

Everyone came running to us as he's the bride's father.

'What happened,' one asked.

'Kya Hua?' someone said.

'Kana heichi?' an old man asked.

'Emindi?' I heard someone from the crowd around me speaking Telugu.

It felt like I was watching a movie in four languages at a time.

'Is there anyone other than these four? Maybe some Tamil and Kannada?' I asked, trying to reduce the heat of the situation.

'Kittii...!' Chitti said, coming towards me.

'Chitti!' I said with relief.

I wanted to hug her and cry because I felt like these people around me would kick me and throw me away.

I'm overreacting right!

Yeah! Actually, I need a reason to hug her. I love her and it's been a while since I met her and a hug is important when you meet your love after a while.

It's such a beautiful feeling to hug your love after a long time. Feeling their presence so close to your heart. It's so comforting as their hair brushes your skin, giving chills all over your body and making you feel there's nothing to worry about.

When I hug her, I feel like our hearts are united as they sound as one. Every time I hug her, I end up whispering I love you in her ear and making her blush. I do so because I love her and she hugs me even tighter and blushes.

'Ishitha beti, do you know him?' the old man behind this entire scene asked.

'Yes uncle,' she smiled. Well, she actually blushed.

'He's calling Chitti and you're calling Kitti. What are those names?' he asked.

'He calls me Chitti because he loves me. He never lets someone call me that way because I'm his love. I call him Kitti because our names rhyme,' Chitti said, grabbing my hand and looking into my eyes.

It's an amazing feeling when the one you love says that you're their love of life in front of everyone. That's so high. We feel the happiness in our eyes that turn into tears making us emotional. That vibe is just beyond expression. Even our breath talks.

Chitti and I became the special attraction at Arpita's wedding.

I found my sister in Arpita and Chitti got a brother in Vijay, Arpita's husband.

*

'Where is Vijay?' I asked Arpita.

'He's the principal now, annaya. So he needs to stay till 5:00 PM. I returned for lunch and stayed back as you're coming,' she said, sipping the tea.

'Thanks a lot, chelli. Now let me go. I need to find Chitti. It's been four days,' I almost cried.

'I'll call Vijay. He'll come with you. These days there are rumours that ivory is being smuggled through Sita Sagar road into Andhra Pradesh. There are raids and people who're new to the place are taken into custody,' Arpita said, dialling Vijay's number.

'I'm already here madam,' Vijay said entering the house with a smile.

'Annaya needs help from you. Can you take him to Sita Sagar now? Be careful,' Arpita said, taking Vijay's bag and giving him water.

'What happened? Why Sita Sagar?' he asked and continued,' I wish Ishitha was also here. You both should come sometime,' he smiled.

'It's an emergency Vijay,' I said and explained everything to him, showing him the letter and the clue I found in the journal. Sita Sagar is the place where my dad has a small place. I found it out a few months ago.

He kept silent. He couldn't accept the truth that Chitti is missing. He feels her like his own sister because she's the only one who tied rakhi to him on Raksha Bandhan for the first time.

'Why do you think she's here? Maybe she's safe. Maybe she is planning to surprise you,' Vijay said. He couldn't think. There were tears in his eyes

'This is the only clue she gave. I should give it a try and this,' I said holding the letter. 'It's the proof for all the things that are happening and it's clear that all this is planned and executed well.' I said determinedly.

'We're finding my sister. Let's go,' Vijay stood up grabbing the car keys.

'Why don't you take police help?' Arpita suggested.

'No chelli! We can't trust anyone now. I told you why,' I got up to leave.

'Take care and stay safe,' she said as we got into the car to leave.

*

'Is this the place?' Vijay whispered as it was on the bank of Sita Sagar and too creepy for someone to even stay there.

'Yes!,' I said, walking slowly ahead of him.

'I think we should wait until it gets dark,' Vijay said.

'No, I don't think there will be more than two people here. I saw my dad and two more guys from Vizag,' I said walking slowly to the door.

There was a crackling sound while I opened the door.

'There's no one,' I signalled Vijay to get in tiptoeing.

There were loads of Elephant trunks. I pulled out my mobile and took a photo.

The sound of my mobile clicking a picture echoed in the room.

'Fuck I forgot to put my mobile on silent,' I said dragging Vijay to the corner behind the heap of trunks.

There were footsteps approaching the room. It was an old man. He seemed familiar to me. He lifted a small trunk and placed it again there leaving the room.

'I think I know him,' I said.

'Let's go and catch that bloody old man,' Vijay said, cracking his fingers.

'But...' before I could say something Vijay ran behind the old man and caught him from behind in such a way that he couldn't shout or move his hands.

In the next few minutes, I searched the house while Vijay handled the old man.

'Dhatree beta?' the old man said as he saw me.

'How do u know me?' I asked him.

'I'm Ramu,' he said.

Ramu was our driver for six years. He was so close to me as he dropped me off at school and drove me anywhere at any time. I don't know what happened to my dad. He suddenly changed the driver and no driver worked for more than six months. My dad eventually got busy with business meetings and never told the reason why he kept changing the drivers.

'What are you doing here?' I asked him.

He had changed completely. His beard wasn't trimmed or shaved in months. His hair crawled up to his neck. He looked like a sadhu living in the Himalayas.

'I'm working with your dad. Don't you know anything about this business?' he asked.

'This is not a business,' I pressed every word that I uttered that resonated in the house.

'This is a business son. This is illegal but this is the biggest business. We earn a lot,' he said proudly as if he's working for the Nation's development.

'You are ruining lives. You took away my love. The love of my life. You are criminals. Where is my Chitti? What did you do to her??' I screamed in my topmost voice.

'Who's she?' he asked as if he didn't know anything.

'She's my life. The one with whom I dreamt of everything in life. What did you do to her? I'm not going to spare any of you. Not you....not my dad,' I uttered each and every word forcing and firing like a bullet.

'You love that journalist?' he asked as if I can't love a journalist.

Chitti is not a journalist, she's a bank employee.

'Where is she now?' Vijay howled at him, giving him a punch.

He pointed to the box in front of him.

I ran to the other end of that room and opened the box.

I was shocked to see the person in the box.

'Vidya?!' I mumbled.

'What?' Vijay said coming towards me.

I fell to my knees. Adrenaline raced and there were thoughts back in my head. This time they're too much to even control. I couldn't resist the rush that made me numb.

My eyes slowly closed and with the setting sun in the west, I fell on the floor motionless.

*

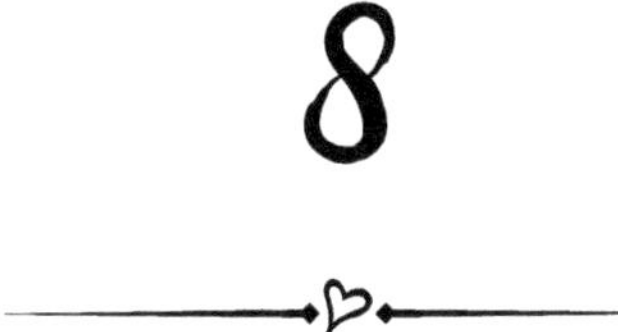

Everything was Black. It's been five days since Chitti is missing and there's no clue about my Chitti.

I woke up with the continuous beep sounds of the pulse monitor.

My Blood pressure kept fluctuating making it difficult for the doctors to do anything. Yes, I needed surgery but I couldn't control my thoughts.

'I don't need the surgery now. I'm fine,' I screamed.

'Annaya you need to calm down,' Arpita Said.

'I can't chelli,' I tried to act normal.

'Dhatree I'll take care of everything now. We're going to find out where Chitti is,' Vidya said entering the room.

Vidya is my friend from my school. It's just been a few months since I met her after eight years.

Sometimes though you live in the same city it takes years to get back to our lost friends. Some school friends never leave. Sooner or later, they find a way to stay than to leave.

She is a journalist. She works for a private news channel in Vizag as a detective journalist. It's been a passion for her since her childhood. The most irritating part is that she talks to us like a journalist. Too many questions. Before you answer one there will be ten more in the line for you waiting to get answered.

People said Vidya was mad and some said she's been in a detective operation for the past two weeks. I called her to tell her that Chitti is missing but her mobile was switched off.

I don't know how she ended up in Paralakhemundi.

'What are you doing here? What happened? Why are you being kidnapped?' I enquired about her.

'I'm in an operation about ivory smuggling and I found out a lot about your father. I already filed a case against him but before it could get into the media, I was kidnapped. I'll tell you everything in detail later. I need to go. I called my channel and asked them to take the court's permission to make a court-hearing shortly,' she said.

'I know about my condition. I can take care. I should go find Chitti,' I said, trying to get up.

If it was a movie I would have ran away from the hospital. It's life. It's reality. I tried to convince Arpita chelli and Vijay as the doctor said I still have one month more and I can go back to Vizag.

Vidya knows that I would do anything to get back Chitti, but she also knows my condition and she agreed with me on one condition that I will have my tablets and update everything to Arpita chelli who is so worried about me.

When something happens to you, your siblings are the ones who care for you and keep an eye on you every second. Yes! Arpita is not related biologically but the bond is strong enough to make her worry about her only brother.

That's how people are these days when you want something you find it in people whom you meet. She found a brother in me while I saw a sister in her.

Vidya and I started off for Vizag that night at 11:00 PM.

Vijay said he'll take care of Ramu until we find Chitti.

I remember the exact time because I miss Chitti every second I breathe.

I don't know if she's safe. I don't know how she came to know about the place Vidya was kept. Smitha is the one who pretended I was sleepy.

I took out the journal from my bag and started to flip the pages slowly.

I came over the first page she wrote.

*

'Today Kitti gifted you to me. Now you're my journal. Well, you're our journal. He wrote how much he loves me. He wrote how much he cares for me and loves me. I asked him to give me something special and he wrote to you last year about the happiness and sadness that we overcame making me love him even more. I love you Dhatree. Don't leave me. Today was special because I just said casually that I want to read his diary, but he made you for me with our memories. What more can I expect than the words he wrote to express and tell how much he loves me. I thought he was showing sympathy as I'm messed up and was in pain with my relationship. People take time to realize reality. I love him. Not just me, everyone loves him. Sometimes that makes me possessive, but I know he's mine. Only mine. He's rare.'

There were tears in my eyes. Without a second thought, I started to read all the pages that she wrote. She wrote her heart out. Putting them in words she made those pages to live with her emotions, some with love, some with anger, some complaining about me. But everything was written with love. She ended every entry with a love symbol. She wrote only about me...she wrote a journal about us. Some made me smile thinking of her innocence, some made me emotional. Some made me think. This was not stressful to my head until I read the last entry..

11/03/2018

'I wish he was with me. I know I'm scared at night, but today was much more different. I saw a horror movie and I can't even go to the restroom now. Now I hate watching horror movies without him. Wait... there's something... What?.... Oh god! It was the curtain. There was a lot to tell you, my journal. I need to tell this to Dhatree soon. His dad is an ivory smuggler. His friend Vidya met me today accidentally and told me to tell Dhatree about the things which were shocking. I thought she was kidding but when she showed me the proof she had, I was shocked. It was a weird day for me. Knowing about Dhatree's dad and my parents leaving me at home alone at night which rarely happens, I fear now for staying alone at my own house as I'm thinking of the horror movie I watched. Why are nights different and so silent? I think I should call him. No, I'm fine, he must be tired. I'll talk a little more to you, my journal.'

'Fear is gripping on me. I wish I had him now. Why the fuck am I hearing weird sounds now out from my house. I need to call him. I'll be back once I check what the sound is and call him. Yes, I fear going down, but the lights are on now. Thank god....'

There was nothing written further. There were tears in my eyes.

I flipped the empty pages. In the end, I found something written.

'Fuucckkkk....!!!!!' I screamed.

Vidya was scared and stopped the car. She looked at me.

I was staring at that page with an angry face. She got down from the car and asked me what happened to pull me out of the car. As I showed her the scribbling at the end of the journal my heart started to pump fast and thoughts raced with a lot of answers and new questions.

*

We're almost at the outskirts of Vizag. I placed my sim card back when we crossed the Orissa border. There was no call from anyone. I kept thinking of how the court session would be that morning.

I dropped Vidya and went back home. I was too tired and it was early in the morning. My father was still awake. As I entered the house my dad hugged me pretending as if nothing happened.

'You'll be fine beta. We'll get you out of this,' he said. There are tears in his eyes. I don't know why he is getting emotional. Maybe because he knows about my epilepsy or maybe he was happy that my Chitti is missing. I went into my room and locked myself in.

Doesn't he know that he needs to attend the court today? Maybe that's the reason he said he'll get me out of this as I don't even know what my dad's business is until last night. I wanted to get some sleep as it's been three days since I had a proper nap.

Throwing my backpack aside I fell on my bed believing that my Chitti is safe. Setting an alarm for 9:00 AM I closed my eyes. My mind was quiet after many days and I slowly drifted off to sleep in seconds. Even in my sleep, the only thought that kept killing me was Chitti. Even the thought that she's no more slowed down my breath. No, nothing could happen to her, my Chitti is safe. I consoled myself.

*

It was difficult for me to wake up because my body was tired and exhausted, but I had to get up. The court hearing is at 11:00 AM and I need to convince my dad that I will act as his lawyer so that I can help him out.

Section 32 of the Advocate's Act clearly mentions, the court may allow any person to appear before it even if he is not an advocate. Therefore, one gets the statutory right to defend one's own case through the Advocate Act in India.

I read this last night online so that I can do a favour for my dad. But, little did I know that within hours my life is going to change.

'We need to go to court?' my dad said as I got down from my room.

'When? I mean why?' I tried to pretend as if I knew nothing.

'There's a case filed against our family. You need not worry about beta. I already called a well-known lawyer,' my dad said, having his tea and reading the newspaper peacefully which I have lacked for the past few days. I mean peace, not the chai and biscuit.

'Dad I can defend us. I mean I want to defend us, there's no need for a lawyer,' I said.

'No, you need not do that. I think that is not allowed,' my dad said, raising his eyes from the newspaper.

'It is allowed dad,' I said sitting in the chair facing him.

'I think you are ready to face things on your own,' he said.

There is not much argument about me defending my dad.

I went up for a bath. The songs played in the background of the shower sound kept reminding me of Chitti. When you love someone their playlist definitely has all the songs you love. We share our playlists and our favourite songs. Now her favourites are mine. Mine are hers. We're different people but our souls are united.

The chill water falling forcefully on my head decreased a bit of pain in my head, relieving my body pains and the sleep that I was not aware of for the past few days. The fear of where Chitti might be and how she might be was still bothering me. Turning off the shower I saw the reflection of my pale face in the mirror.

'You need to do this to find Chitti. You'll be fine. Why don't you focus on what and how you need to talk at the court,' I told myself.

Walking out of the bathroom I kept thinking of how I should argue. I have proof and facts that need to be shown. I also need to protect my dad.

Should I?

'I need to do this,' I said to myself as I got into the car. Dad and mom are already waiting in the car.

'Why are you, nervous son? Everything will be fine. No one can stop your marriage,' my dad said, patting my back.

'Marriage?'

Who talks about marriage when the girl I want to share my life with has been missing for the past week. Nice acting dad, you did everything and you are acting as if you know nothing. I hope you get an Oscar if you act in movies. This is the life you need to know the difference.

Maybe I should have known about the trap that was already waiting for me.

The court was about to start. I don't know why Varsha's parents are here. Maybe to see my dad. I don't know what kind of parents they are.

It's been two days since Varsha was not home and they are not even bothered about how and where she is. Great parents.

'Dhatree come and stand in the bone,' the person beside the judge called me.

Me?

I was supposed to stand beside my dad who will be in the cage and defend him right?

'Everything will be fine,' my dad said as I looked at him not knowing what was happening.

I slowly walked into the wooden cage that was older than my age. Staring at the stranger who is looking at me as if I'm an accused in a rape case. I turned to the judge who controlled the murmurings with a single bang of a wooden hammer.

'Order... Order..' the person in his early sixties banged the wooden hammer on his table commanding everyone. ' I'm the judge here and you need to do what I say.' Just the banging sounds of the hammer told me a lot for the first time.

Maybe you get to know a few things with experience which you can't get by seeing movies. Most of the time, we use 'Maybe' just to say some truths that we are not confident in accepting.

'Mr. Dhatree, there's an allegation against you that you are engaged with Varsha, daughter of Mr Sharma and due to some issue you disagreed and kidnapped her a day ago,' he said in his husky voice.

'What the fuck!' I screamed aloud.

'Order... Order... You should not use unparliamentary language here. This is the court,' he said.

'I am sorry sir. I thought this was the case with my dad. I was not engaged to anyone. I've been in love with a girl for the past two years and we wanted to get married. Though Varsha and her parents asked about marrying her a month ago I politely denied it. I didn't kidnap her,' I said and he kept listening keenly to every line I said.

My head started to ache as I kept thinking of why would Varsha's parents file a case against me and why my parents didn't let me know anything about the case. Before the judge could tell anything the lawyer whom Varsha's family hired got up to make his point.

'My lord. The accused Mr Dhatree trapped my client Varsha and had a physical relationship with her for a month. She loved him so she agreed to everything he said. But Mr Dhatree just used her for his desires....' before he could say anything more.

'BC he's lying. I didn't even meet her without my friend Raghav. Fuck you,' I screamed with anger. The biggest mistake I made was yelling at him. But, I couldn't control my anger. My head was heating up with the thought of where is Chitti? What's happening to my life? I did nothing wrong and now I have false allegations against me.

I signalled Vidya for my tablets who were staring at me not knowing what was happening.

She came running to me with a water bottle and my tablets. I saw the change of expressions on my dad's face as he saw her and that too with me. Though he's my dad he doesn't know anything about the friends I have. He was so busy with business. Maybe busy covering the illegal things in his business.

'My lord with due respect, I'm addressing him as Mr. Dhatree and he uses unparliamentary language to address me. I want him to apologize before I continue with the remaining things,' the lawyer said.

'Mr. Dhatree you need to control yourself and talk politely. This is the court. You are an accused until it's proven that you are not,' the Judge said.

'Sir I'm sorry but I'm not aware that there was a case filed against me. I didn't do anything to Varsha,' I said.

'My lord, the Accused has promised my client that he'll marry her and when the date of engagement was approaching, he said he had a girlfriend and that he wanted to marry her. Here are the proofs about the invitation for the engagement. The pictures of my client with him. My client was also missing for the past 24 hours. When we checked her call list, Mr Dhatree was the last person she called at 1:00 AM yesterday. He kidnapped her. His mobile was switched off yesterday and he got back home this morning. The proof that he kidnapped her was that both my clients and Mr Dhatree's mobiles were at a place when her mobile was switched off. He kidnapped her, my lord. I want you to punish this person who uses women for his desires and later leaves them,' the lawyer said out loud, taking his seat.

I was clueless about how they clearly framed everything according to their plan. I was stuck. My head started to hurt as I kept thinking.

'Mr. Dhatree, Is there anything you want to say?' the judge asked me.

I was silent. I was numb. What should I say? I was prepared for my dad's case and I ended up here not knowing what to do or what to say.

'Mr. Dhatree, Is there anything you have to say?' the judge banged the hammer asking for my attention.

'Yes sir,' I said looking at him.

'Proceed,' he started to gaze at me.

'Sir I didn't kidnap Varsha. She's the sister of my best friend Raghav. She proposed to me a month ago and her parents talked to my mother. She said that she would talk to my father once he returned from his business trip. I told her about the girl I love and we denied the proposal of Varsha's family. My friend, Raghav, tried to convince me to marry Varsha and Varsha herself asked me a lot of times. My answer was always a 'No'. I don't know about the engagement or anything else sir. Varsha called me that night as my girlfriend was missing and she said that she found something. She's safe sir. She was given a high dosage of Cocaine so she was not well. She's getting treated. You can ask her everything sir,' I said.

'Mr. Dhatree we need proof for everything you said. Why didn't you inform her parents about Varsha ?' the judge asked.

'Because her father is a drug dealer..' I said.

'Objection my lord,' the lawyer said and continued.

'My lord Mr Dhatree doesn't have any proof and is taking the case in the wrong direction. My client is a well-known businessman and is known all over the state. Now Mr Dhatree is trying to defame my client's reputation,' he said in such a confident way as if that's the truth.

'Mr. Dhatree, do you have any proof?' the judge asked.

'Sir I'm not a lawyer but can I ask you something?' I said.

'Go on,' the judge smiled for the first time.

'I don't even know what the case is, sir. I'm not in a state to explain now. Can you give me a day time so that I can give you every possible proof about the case,' I pleaded.

'Are you sure you'll provide the evidence by tomorrow?' the judge asked.

'Yes sir,' I said confidently, thinking of things I was not even clear about.

'Okay, then the court is giving you a day time. Tomorrow is the third Saturday and the court will work as usual. Now the court is adjourned,' he said, getting up to leave.

'Sir, can I ask you one thing?' I said, still standing on the wooden bone while everyone started to leave.

'Yes! Mr Dhatree,' he smiled standing near his chair.

'Sir I don't know what's happening in my life. I am in search of my love who has been missing for the past six days. I found a lot. People whom I thought were mine are not even telling me anything or telling the truth. I don't know if I can prove my innocence. But sir, I promise you that I will unmask some big secrets and you'll be smiling the same way for giving the verdict,' I smiled.

He smiled and left.

I felt like a hero of a movie as BGM played at the back. Maybe that's the reason they say 'Heroes are not born, they are made. Everyone is a hero.'

Maybe that's how we learn life. I mean in hardships, our guts get stronger as we get to know what we have and what we need to do. We might be confused at first but we get the confidence when we know we are not at fault. Not everyone who has a case on them is a criminal. There will be a cause and reason behind every case.

*

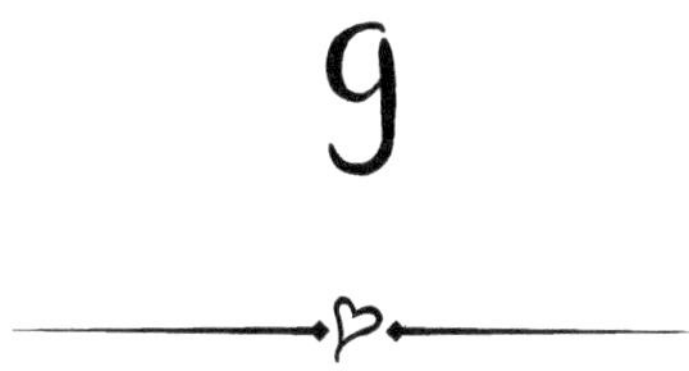

I took permission from the court to collect the evidence like video footage and a few other things that only the police department has access to. It all depends on the rules in the 'Right to Information Act.'

I have very few people now. My family is eliminated from the things they did. Raghav was long gone. Varsha is the one who can help me. I should talk to her but I think they'll be spying on me. Maybe no because the words I said after the court gives them the confidence that I'll be trapped forever.

My mom and dad called me after the court hearing. 'My case is after lunch. Will you stay?' he asked as if nothing happened to my life that's about to get ruined.

Before he could put his hand on my shoulder I stopped him.

Displaying my anger in my eyes that turned red and started watering for the reason that my parents are also the reason behind this. I screamed, 'Well planned. I felt nothing knowing that my own parents want me to suffer for things I didn't do. Great parents.'

I walked away to the parking lot before I fell unconscious.

I wished my parents would be there by my side when I woke up, but I'm wrong. Why will they be beside me when they're busy getting some fake proof to prove my dad is innocent.

Vidya was there beside me. The only one who can help me now. It's been half an hour since I passed away in the parking lot.

Vidya saw me as she followed me to talk after my talk with my parents. She took me to our house as she knows I have epilepsy. Maybe I'm the only epilepsy patient in the world who falls unconscious too many times thinking too much.

'What to do now?' she asked, looking at me.

She knows I'll not rest. She knows how desperate I'm to find my love, Chitti.

I smiled at her asking for my mobile.

I called Chandrika.

'Hello!!'

'Varsha is fine. Don't worry,' she said before I could ask her anything.

That's what I've been asking her for the past day so she got habituated to answer the same.

'I need to talk to you. I'll send you the location, come there along with Varsha,' I said.

'Vidya, you take this paper and collect the CCTV footage at the hospital that I'm admitted into and also the CCTV footage at Chitti's house. Call me once you are done. I'll send you the location,' I said, packing my clothes, my medicines and belongings in a trolley.

'What are you doing? Where are you leaving,' she asked.

'To the place where the people called mine can enter anytime,' I smiled.

'You need to talk to your parents, you mean the world to them. Maybe there's a reason for them to do this. Things will get better. Just talk to them,' Vidya said.

'Can I tell you one thing?' I asked her.

'What now?' she said, staring at me.

'Do you know why they did and what they did to me?' I asked, staring away.

'I know Dhatree but they are your parents,' she tried to convince.

'Vidya you don't know what they did. Yes! That's what I'm saying, they are my parents. At least they have to stay by my side on the days I'm leftover by the world and that time is now. Where are they? They are not here and the reason for this is them, Vidya. You don't know them. I know them totally and yes they did this all with the help of an asshole. I need to go. If you don't want to stay on my side you can...... I'm fine with all this. I know what to do,' I said, picking up my bags and the paper from her hands getting out of my house.

She came to me slowly thinking what would have happened. I couldn't tell her totally because I don't know if it's true.

'Dhatree,' she whispered slowly.

'What?' I said. Coldness filled my words.

When you don't have someone to control you, your words become cold. They reflect your love on them, as you don't want them to get hurt because of you. But understanding that does matter. And, when they understand they stay by your side. Ever after.

'Where should I keep the keys?' she asked.

'Throw them away,' I wanted to scream.

But, what if my parents don't have a spare key. I'm still thinking of them, but do they? I don't want to think much.

'Keep it in the post box,' I said as I got into the car.

'At least now, will you give me the permission letter to get the CCTV footage?' she asked as she got into the car.

'I'll drop you and leave,' I said, igniting the engine.

'Where will you go?' she asked.

'To the place where I can see her,' I smiled looking at her and accelerating the car.

*

Things started to fall in place. After dropping Vidya, I went to Raghav's house.

I knew there would be guards at the entrance so I went behind his house where he used to jump in, at midnight to sneak in. He's caught once but it's his house.

It was a duplex house with a swimming pool at the back and a gym on the top floor.

No one was home. They might be busy covering their illegal activities of cocaine trafficking. You might be wondering why am I telling you all this without any proof and without finding my Chitti.

I'm looking for Chitti. I'm just a few metres away from her. I want to hug her tight and cry in her arms. I should have been a few minutes earlier that night.

I know that there are CCTV cameras there but I need to take a risk. I don't have any other option. I need to find Chitti. Walking slowly to the back door observing the surroundings I sneaked into the house.

The back door was always open because of the kitchen that is attached to it. Servants come and leave. I slowly walked up the stairs to the room no one was allowed to enter.

Raghav's dad warned Raghav as he once tried to sneak in late. The alarm rang bringing everyone there back then. I know the technology is updated now. So I need to find a new way. It was a fingerprint lock. I saw in a lot of movies that we can see the fingerprint.

I had less time. I slowly walked into the room attached to the secret room searching for talcum Powder and a makeup brush. I ran to the drawing-room for a tape and came back. It's already 1:00 PM. The court might have started. I have only a few more minutes, that's it. I put some power in the lock and slowly brushed the surface. Carefully I placed the tape over the Power tracing the fingerprint. It's not a thumb finger. I placed my finger tracing the fingerprint into the scanner.

There was a sound and the door opened.

I entered the room and felt numb. It was not just a room. It's a vault for cocaine storage. I stood there thinking what I should do. Suddenly there was a car sound that caught my attention. I understood that someone was home.

*

'The court session is in a few more minutes, are you nervous?' Vidya asked.

'Yes! I am. But don't worry things will be fine,' I said more to myself.

'So Mr Dhatree did you get the proof,' the Judge asked, adjusting his spectacles.

'Sir I request that no one should interrupt me while talking. You can ask me anything once I'm done. With all due respect I also request you also Mr Lawyer, not to object to me,' I said determined with the reddish eyes that have been sleepless for the past week.

Anger is not on the people around me. It's towards my people.

'I agree Mr Dhatree,' the Judge said, for which Mr Lawyer also agreed by nodding his head.

'Sir let me tell you about the facts like a story. Everyone loves to listen to stories right! My story is to tell you the actual truth,' I said, signalling Vidya to come with all the evidence.

'Sir, I love Ishitha. The girl who's confident and passionate. It's been two years since we're in love. I have known her for three years. Our parents accepted our love and we wanted to get settled before we got married. This one week changed everything. You might be wondering what happened. Last weekend she called me to say that something wrong was happening at her place. She wanted me to come. I was exhausted but I should take care of her. I took my bike and raced to her house. When I was about to reach her house, my head felt drowsy and suddenly a girl came onto me. I fell off as I instantly applied the brakes. Seeing her come running to me my eyes slowly got closed and I went unconscious. I woke up in a hospital after two days. The doctor said that I hit a pole and that I got epilepsy. Varsha was there with me. She told me that Chitti was kidnapped. I enquired in the hospital where I was admitted. They said a girl joined me and left, telling me that she'll come back but she didn't,' I paused.

Everyone's eyes in the court kept staring at me. Few people are excluded though.

'Why are you telling all this,' the judge asked.

'Sir you need the truth, let me explain everything,' I said and continued.

'I went to the PS along with Varsha who agreed to be my well-wisher and best friend like Raghav. There I met Aditya, Ishitha's cousin. He's investigating her case. As per the clues I'm one of the suspects as my footprints are in her house. Along with one other footprint. To my surprise before I could explain anything he said that I'm not the suspect. Trying to remember about that night I fainted at the place I met with the accident. I woke up in Ishitha's house with her mother beside me. I came across the ivory carving on the shelf and memorized the words of the girl who came running to me that night of the accident. 'Ivory' She said ivory and that girl is Smita,' I said, recalling everything.

'Varsha, Aditya and I went to her house and asked her what happened that night. As I called her and asked her to check on Chitti before I could reach her she went and saw Ishitha arguing with someone. Seeing Smita, Chitti asked her to run away. That's how she hit my vehicle that night. She also said she can recognise the second person. Aditya said he'll arrange a sketch artist. Varsha and Aditya left while I stayed to drink water. Smita gave me a journal saying that Chitti gave her that night after scribbling something and she warned me, 'Don't let anyone know about this, not even the people with you.' That night while searching for a clue in the diary I got a call from Varsha. She cut the call telling her she knew something about Chitti. She called again from an unknown number. She was in a panic telling me she was running towards my house. I felt like the same scene of Chittii was being repeated. I took my car and drove to Varsha's house. On the way, I saw her running and stopped the car. She came running and fell in front of me. There was a bullet in her back. I took her to my friend's house. She first declined but later I convinced her to treat Varsha. I went home and while flipping through the pages of the journal, I found a strange note that looked mysterious. I later decoded it as 'Your dad is a drug dealer. He hates me. Paralakhemundi Sita Sagar.' I packed my bag and went to Paralakhemundi lying to my parents that I'm going to Hyderabad,' I saw my father's face shocked.

'In Paralakhemundi, I found that my dad is an ivory smuggler and he kidnapped Vidya. She found this and told Chittii before she went missing. I was back last morning and got into this false allegation that framed me as a criminal.'

'Sir these are the pictures that I took in Paralakhemundi. The trunks are stocked up in huge numbers. And, my sim was switched off for a day sir but not my Whatsapp. I kept everything updated to my friend Chandrika. Here are the reports from AIIMS Hyderabad that Varsha is given a high dosage of cocaine,' I said, submitting the reports to the judge.

'Varsha.!' I called out.

She slowly walked out from the crowd taking off her scarf.

'Did I use you for my wants and promised to marry?' I asked.

'No sir. Dhatree is a good friend of mine. It's all the plan of my dad. I loved Dhatree but he never crossed his line. He was committed to Ishitha. Here are the bills for my engagement cards. I'm so sorry Dhatree,' she said with tears.

'Objection my lord,' the lawyer came out.

'Sir, I told you not to interrupt until I'm done,' I said.

'Objection overruled. Please continue Mr Dhatree,' the judge said.

'Sir, Can you check the date on which the order is given for the cards. That too fifty cards are given. Mr Sharma is a well-known person all over the state and he just gave fifty cards. That too just a day before the case was filed. Which was two days ago. It's a point to be noted, sir. These are the pictures I took at Varsha's house. It's a cocaine vault. And, the second footprint. It's Mr Raghav Sharma. He's the one who kidnapped my Chitti. I found her in Mr Sharma's house in that vault. She's given drugs that keep her alive but unconscious for a maximum of twenty-four hours. She was given the dosage every twenty-four hours,' there were tears in my eyes.

'Smita told me everything that Mr Sharma and Mr Raghav Sharma had plotted. You created a nice story,' I said looking at them forcing every word I uttered. There was anger and tears mixed up in my eyes that evaporates before it could get out.

'Smita was blackmailed and Mr Aditya had a lot of pressure as Mr Sharma has a lot of influence. That's the reason the sketch she described was my dad's but not yours, Mr Raghav Sharma.'

'Sir, Mr Sharma wanted me to marry his daughter no matter what. When Varsha said 'No' to his plan on the day of my discharge, he was angry and wanted to convince her. She didn't agree and said she'll say everything to me. He couldn't bear it and slapped her. She maintains two mobiles. One was hers and the other was a gift from her brother. She was given cocaine through an injection. But, she was a drug addict once so she resisted for a while. Mr Sharma somehow managed to shoot her. He thought she's dead.'

'Raghav likes Chitti. So if I'm married to his sister then he can marry Chitti. But, that will happen only if I marry Varsha. That's the reason they kidnapped Chitti. They thought they'd convince me that Chittii is dead and make me marry Varsha but it didn't work out.'

'What actually happened that night was, Chitti took me to her house with the help of Smita. That's how my footprints are there. They called an ambulance but it was getting late. So Smita went to her house to bring her car. In the meantime, Mr Sharma came to talk to Chitti along with Raghav. She said 'no' to everything they said. She took the journal and came to me. I was on the couch. They pretended as if they left but they came back and tried to take her away from me who's holding my hand. She shouted for help but no one came. That's when Raghav hit me on my head as I tried to move a bit. Smita saw everything who came there by that time. 'Take him to the hospital,' Chitti screamed. That's the reason she went back to see what happened to Chitti. But no one was there. She saw the journal that was thrown on the floor and read everything. The next day Mr Sharma went to Smita's house and threatened her not to say anything. Aditya was beside him but was helpless. That's the reason why he said that I'm not a suspect in the first place.'

'Chittii wrote everything in the journal. Here is a copy of that sir. She knows about my dad, about them not liking me and her to get married and about Mr Sharma's business. She knows everything except the fact that they had a big plan behind it. But now she's in the hospital,' I said.

'Hospital? What?!' the judge asked.

'Sir, she's fine. She's under-diagnosis,' I tried to act normal.

'Sir this is the video of a family affected by this cocaine addiction. The evidence I gave you will prove my innocence and make strong evidence for the two illegal businesses. Aditya, Thanks for the letter you kept in my car,' I smiled.

'Aditya knew everything about Mr Sharma. He discussed the case with Chitti and asked if I could help as I'm Raghav Sharma's friend. But, before she could tell any of it she...' my voice trailed off.

It was very clearly seen in everyone's face, the sympathy for me. There was fear in my dad's and Mr Sharma's face.

A verdict was given. There was another investigation on my father and Mr Sharma and was carried out by Aditya transparently. They're proven guilty and sent to jail.

You might be wondering what about the car that stopped when I was at Mr Sharma's house.

It's Varsha and Chandrika. Chandrika texted me once she collected the information. I sent her my location. Varsha stayed back at her house to make sure that no one would know that I found Chitti. And, she also assured her parents that she'll marry me so that they would believe her.

*

' Dhatree...! Ishitha...!' someone's voice ended my thoughts.

'Someone is here,' Chitti said, opening the door.

' I'm here with good news,' Varsha said walking into the backyard.

' It's been a while, madam. How are you?' I asked.

' I'm good. There's good news for all of us,' she said with a twinkle in her eyes.

' Are you going to have a baby or what?' Chitti said, sitting beside me.

'Hush!!! Our business is going to expand. I got a call from an investor. He directly wants to invest. I said 'no' to him as our business is at its peak and we ourselves have money to expand it. And, why are you guys so bothered about my baby, think of yours first? I want to play with my little Dhatree,' she smiled.

'Your little Dhatree. Acha!!' I winked.

'Ha... I want a boy,' she smiled.

'But, I want a baby girl,' I looked at Chitti.

'Very good. Now shut up,' Chitti pinched my nose.

Varsha married Aditya as he proposed to her a few months ago. She left her house and started to stay with us for a while until she got married. We started a business called 'Vihaar'.

It's a small start-up that provides tours for little places all over our state. Basically, there are a lot of places that are left unexplored. We are like a consultancy to the people who want to travel. We give information to the people who want to travel and get them connected to the people near the places they want to explore.

'Can't you talk to your parents?' Varsha asked.

It's been eleven months since I talked to them. Almost a year. I was angry with them for not being there for me. I was not actually angry. I was in pain when they said they wanted me to marry Varsha. The reason that they said kept me distressed. Money. That's what they said.

I don't know why people have this greed to become richer. I never loved money because I'm already in love with my Chittii and I always dreamt of becoming a businessman who sees life and business separately.

When you mix life and business, you can only see business. Even illegal things become legal.

'I asked you not to talk about that again,' I said, raising my voice.

Chittii came and sat beside me, tightening her grip on my shoulder and she insisted on cooling down.

I looked at her thinking of how hard things were for us when we started our life together.

There's a lot of life we have seen in the past few months. The difficulties of starting a business. We lacked support. Handling Chitti during her diagnosis was difficult for me. My epilepsy operation was done and my condition was getting better with time. There was a lot of pain. The pain people can see in the way we behave. Chitti's parents tried to help out but the absence of my own parents bothered me. That was the past and the future for us is promising.

My epilepsy is long gone. The more I think now the better I make my life with the ideas I get. Life teaches us everything. How to heal and how to live.

It's all about how we take it. Some people try to stay and some might want to leave. Let's believe they'll turn around someday as my parents did.

They came back for us after a few months. I couldn't talk but I didn't disrespect them. Some lessons make us strong, some make us think. I got both.

Mr Sharma and my dad were on bail. The first thing they did was come to our house and ask us to forgive and forget the past.

Forgetting is not the part of the time that passes. We can never forget things that hit us hard. I forgave them but I can never forget.

'Bhayya, she wants to meet you,' one of my employees said.

'Who?' I asked him Busy at work.

A little girl came walking into my cabin with a shiny face and a glittery smile.

'Ishitha,' I said, getting up with a smile, going close to her.

She's the little girl whose dad is once a drug addict and now an employee in my office. He's a B.Tech passed out, but worked under a contract for a minimum daily wage.

'My dad never leaves me now,' she said.

I took her closer to my heart and hugged her smiling. Tears rolled down from my eyes.

*

"Ends are always happy unless you make one. Believe in yourself.

-Dhatree Suneeth."

"'Believe in your heart that you're meant to live a life full of passion, purpose, magic and miracles.'

- Roy T. Bennett."

About The Author

Dhatree Suneeth Maradana is a Telugu-born writer who comes from a middle-class family. He was grown and brought up in Vijayawada, Andhra Pradesh. While pursuing his engineering at Velagapudi Ramakrishna Siddhartha engineering college in Vijayawada, he found his interest in writing. In 2018, he started posting his work on Instagram on his public page called dha3s_writeups. Soon he received appreciation and more people became fond of his writings. He further enhanced his creativity by publishing some short stories in Wattpad namely: The confused love story, That Week, 7 PM walk, A managed 22, Someone interesting. These short stories are based on many emotions, in which he expresses unbearable pain with his words. The mature love stories that flow from him are so heart-touching that readers often end up with tiny drops of water in the corner of their eyes.

He draws his inspiration from the motivation given his father. He is 24 now and is currently pursuing Masters in Business Administration from GITAM University (Vizag). He got through his first novel (A STORY OF MINE) by taking short breaks while making progress on his interest in writing. It has been an exquisite journey for him while writing this novel.

He has gone through every emotion in his real life, which he frames into sentences that captivate your mind and heart as you read this book. He is a good human being with a kind heart and rage under control. He is no different than us but he succeeded in finding his passion and loves helping others with his words.

9 798887 172477

Printed by Libri Plureos GmbH in Hamburg,
Germany